Neekna and Chemai

Jeannette C. Armstrong

Illustrated by Barbara Marchand

Library and Archives Canada Cataloguing in Publication

Armstrong, Jeannette C.

Neekna and Chemai / by Jeannette Armstrong ; illustrated by

Barbara Marchand.

ISBN 978-1-894778-56-5

1. Indians of North America--British Columbia--Juvenile fiction.

I. Marchand, Barbara II. Title.

PS8551.R7635N4 2007   jC813'.54   C2007-907484-7

Printed in China by Everbest Printing

THEYTUS BOOKS
www.theytus.com

We acknowledge the support of the Canada Council for the Arts. We also
acknowledge the support of the Province of British Columbia through the British
Columbia Arts Council.

Neekna and Chemai

Jeannette C. Armstrong

Illustrated by Barbara Marchand

THEYTUS BOOKS

Chapter 1
WINTER

"Chemai, get up! It's morning, come and play with me," I shouted to my best friend. I knew it wasn't polite to shout, but on a morning like this, a big fat shout was just waiting to be let out. "Hurry up and look at the snow; there's a thick pile of it everywhere, hiding everything. There are even tracks of our animal relatives. They must have visited us early and became tired of waiting."

Chemai answered with a sleepy yawn, "Okay, Neekna, I'll get up, but I know you always make up big stories just to tease me." Boy, was Chemai surprised! I hadn't made this story up; it was just as I said. We ran around like happy squirrels, chattering, laughing and throwing snow at each other. Pretty soon, my grandmother came from our underground lodge.

"Come in, Neekna, your mother has a meal ready. You may come too, Chemai. We have some berries and meat. This snow is very beautiful, isn't it?"

My family was already sitting at eating mats when we climbed down from outside. It was warm in the underground lodge. My two brothers and other sister were also sitting down. Everyone talked while we ate.

My father said, "Today my sons will track rabbits and make snares. I will show them where to put them. Tonight we will eat roast rabbit."

My mother nodded and said, "Today my mother and daughters will work in the big house. We will finish weaving the mats and bags that we need for the hop-dance."

My grandpa said, "Today I will continue my teaching of the older boys. We will make more spears and arrow tips. It is hard work, but we will need many for hunting this summer."

After we had eaten the morning meal, we went over to the big earth house. We looked at the work the older girls and women were doing while we waited for tule and hemp to weave with. There were some huge baskets woven from coils of slender cedar roots. These had pretty designs.

Chemai said, "Look at this big *tule* mat my grandma is weaving. It will be a new covering for our summer tipi." It was big. Other women were tanning hides, which were stretched out on square frames made of logs.

One of my aunts was busy making some new clothing and moccasins. She had laid the skins out and was cutting the pieces she needed with a sharp flint knife.

"Come on, Chemai," I said. "Let's make a fire in our play-tipi." Some of the other girls had already made a nice warm fire by the time we arrived.

"Hi Neekna, Hi Chemai," they said. Everyone began talking about the new snow and the animal tracks. As we sat down to work, a very tiny old lady with a cane came in. Everyone jumped up to greet her. She was our favourite person.

She knew how to be very funny. She made us laugh and feel happy everytime we saw her. We hugged her and almost dragged her to the best seat next to the fire on the soft bear robe.

"Hi Tupa, are you visiting all morning?"
In our language, *Tupa* means great-grandparent.
"Would you tell us some stories?"
"Do you want some hot cherry-top tea?"
Tupa laughed. She was so tiny that
she was our size. Some said Tupa
had seen over a hundred snows!

"Yes, I'll have some tea," said Tupa. "No, I'll not tell a story today. Yes, I will visit all morning. I have some things to tell you. You are my little chickadee girls. I want you to grow up to be as beautiful as the red-winged mountain birds." After Tupa sat down, we covered her up with our fur robes. We knew she got cold easily. We gave her some hot tea in a tiny basket that was woven very tight to hold the liquid in.

"Tomorrow there will be visitors from another village," she said.
"We are going to have a dance. I will tell you about that." We sat very quietly, weaving while she talked.

"All things big and small move in a big circle, even the times we call winter, spring, summer and fall. One always comes back to winter as each year starts again. Winter is preparation time. It is during the moons of winter that we make clothing, tools, baskets and weapons for the next season. It is time to get things ready for the coming seasons.

It is the same with those things we cannot see, but which are there just the same. Can you see a song? Can you see the wind? No, but when a person sings, you can see his smile. When the wind blows, you can see the flowers nod their heads."

Tupa said, "The things we prepare at winter dances are things you cannot see, but what it brings, you can see. Your mothers and fathers, aunts, uncles and the old people pray at these dances.

They pray for the health and well-being of every one of their relatives in the coming seasons. They pray for lots of food to grow in the seasons of gathering. They dance and dance. They ask for lots of snow, so there will be lots of good moisture for the plants to grow in the spring and summer. The animals and birds will have plenty of food and so will we."

Tupa's voice was so soft as she said, "So it has been for all time, since we were formed as people of this land. When lots of people dance hard, everything grows well and there is plenty for every living thing. That is the way the Great Creator Spirit showed the people, so we can live without hardship. Everything will die and diseases eat up all living things if we do not live according to the plan of the Great Spirit. You must remember that always. You must carry these things I tell you to your great-grandchildren."

Our great-grandma then finally did tell us
a teeny-weeny story. She told us about the time a
little boy went out with this dog to look for squirrel
food caches.

"Once, long ago, there was a little boy who
was hungry for pine nuts. He knew he could find
some if he located the squirrel caches.

This little boy left without his stiff fur leg-
wraps. The snow wasn't very deep and he left his
snowshoes, too. He walked with his dog looking
for squirrel tracks. Finally, he saw some and they
hurriedly followed the tracks.

He could just taste the pine nuts.
As he was walking, the tracks became
bigger and bigger. Finally, they were
nearly as big as his dog tracks. Suddenly
he realized that something was wrong.
He hadn't noticed before, but now the
sun hid behind grey clouds and Little
Wind (who was a brother to Sky) pushed
puffs of snow around.

The little boy stopped and said,
"Come my puppy, let's turn and follow
our tracks home." As he turned, he heard
laughter and someone said, "Look at the
foolish boy, he follows any old tracks."

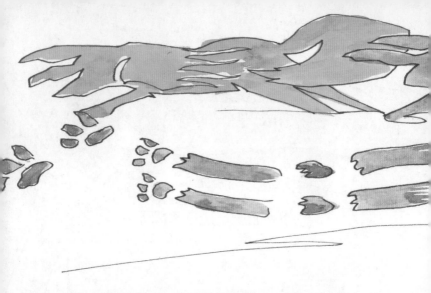

It was the North Wind. Tracks that were made by Squirrel, then Rabbit, then Coyote had played tricks on the little boy. They were asked to do this by North Wind. He wanted to whip the little boy for being disrespectful by not wearing the proper clothing while walking in the woods. North Wind hurled some icy snow at the little boy, stinging his hands and face.

"Go home!" he roared. "I am too mean for disrespectful little boys to be walking without warm leg-wraps and snowshoes." North Wind didn't want to hurt the little boy, but he wanted him to learn to dress respectfully when he went out where the North Wind was.

If he didn't learn, the next time he would be punished worse; maybe North Wind would bite his fingers and toes.

"The little boy and his dog ran all the way home, arriving there just as it was getting dark. They had gone a long way from home. They were so cold when they finally got into their tent-house they were almost stiff."

Tupa told us to remember this story. I knew we would. We were all afraid of the North Wind, his songs sounded scary, as he whipped fine snow-dust in piles around our lodge.

Chapter 2
SPRINGTIME

"Neekna, Neekna!" Chemai shouted, her voice sounding far away. "Come and see the buttercups." I ran to the hillside where Chemai was walking with her grandmother. There were bright yellow flowers scattered all over the grey ground. Little brown streams of melted snow water trickled everywhere. Up higher, the hilltops were still covered with white. This was the first moon of spring. We had a lot of fun that day playing on the warm hillside facing the sun. We talked to the buttercups and they smiled up at us.

"Hello my friends, how good it is to see you again," I said. "I'm glad you are back because you bring the warm sun with you." The buttercups just smiled and smiled.

Soon the green leaf moon was shining. My grandma sat with me and said, "Tomorrow, we will walk along the shale banks to find the green plant that grows before all other food. It is a medicine. Your stomach has been used to dried food all winter along. Now in the seasons to come, fresh foods will be plenty."

"This green plant tells your stomach to get ready for all the fresh foods you will be eating, so your stomach will not sicken and you will live many years."

My grandma seemed to know everything. I wondered how she got to know all that.

"Grandma, I found a big one! Look!" I gave grandma the big green plant I had found. She smiled and I ran to find some more. A lot of our people were walking around and we had fun shouting and laughing and sliding down the slippery shale banks. Although they couldn't climb very high, even the old ones were out.

"Tupa," I shouted, "Come up here! There's lots up here! Do you want us to help you up?" Great-grandma leaned on her cane and laughed.

"Oh, I can run all the way to the top. I did, just a while ago when you weren't looking, but now I'm tired."

Chemai said, "Wow, I wish we had been watching." We sat by Tupa to eat our medicine plant while she sang a pretty song. She said she was happy because she was here, too.

One day, not long after the green leaf time, father talked to us. He said, "The bitterroot will soon be ready to dig. Tomorrow we will move to our spring camp to dig bitterroot at White Lake."

Chemai and I were very excited about going. She ran to me. "Come Neekna, let's not forget to take our baskets." We had lots of fun running back and forth to the big bundles our mothers were making. We watched the men make big round rolls out of the tule mats that would be used for covering our summer homes. There was so much work and excitement.

The sun was very warm as we started out to White Lake. There were lots of people and horses. The horses had bundles tied to their backs. Some horses carried the old; old ones like Tupa. Tupa called down to us, "Look at me, I feel like a bird way up here." She flapped her arms around and said, "Caw-caw," like a crow. We laughed and walked alongside her horse.

"Look, Chemai, there is White Lake. Look at all the camps! There are lots and lots of people." We ran ahead towards the campgrounds. Out across the sagebrush, you could see many people bent over digging. Many were small girls our age.

While our fathers and brothers put up the mat tipis, our mothers made fires and cooked. We were very hungry. We hadn't eaten all day, except for the handfuls of dried berries we carried in pouches tied to our belts.

"Mmmmm, the dried fish soup smells so good," Tupa said, "I could eat until I looked like a mosquito."

My mother laughed. "You already look like a mosquito Tupa, only now you will look like a full mosquito." Tupa laughed and made a humming sound and began to sing. Her voice was like a mosquito's too, but her song was pretty. She sang and all the women sang with her. We knew they were all happy to be at the root digging camp and thankful that the roots were plentiful.

During that moon, we dug so much bitterroot that we had sacks and sacks of it. I helped my grandmother gather the dried ones we had spread out on rush mats the day before. I asked, "Tupa, why did we eat all the bitterroot we dug the first day; why didn't we dry that too?"

She answered, "It is because we celebrate with the first ones we dig. We thank the spirit of Bitterroot for giving us his body to eat. Bitterroot was a Chief a long time ago, before we people came to be. He was kind. When he heard that we would be coming to live on this land, he knew we could not get food like he does. He eats dirt."

So he said, "I will give my body up and it will grow in special places for these helpless ones to use when they come."

The Great Spirit said, "That is kind of you, Chief Bitterroot. When the people come, you will always be honoured at feasts. Your people will never forget you."

"How could anyone ever forget Chief Bitterroot?" I thought after grandma told me that. I was glad he had made his body into food for us. No wonder Bitterroot was so beautiful. The Creator must have been pleased with him.

Chapter 3
SUMMERTIME

"Come on, Chemai, you are getting too slow," I said, "We will soon be at the saskatoon berry picking place." I knew Chemai was tired; we all were. Besides, it was hot on this day of travelling during the saskatoon berry moon. We were on our way to a spot near the Great Bluff to pick the good saskatoons. This place is near the Inkameep camps. It seemed to be a long way from White Lake. All the horses swished their tails as they walked slowly along. Pretty soon we could see the big bluff near where we would camp. It would be nice to sit down. My feet were beginning to feel very tired.

"Here, Neekna, come and sit beside me," grandma said. "I have some pieces of dried meat we can chew on while we are waiting for the tipis to be put up and your mother to cook supper." My grandma sure was nice. It was good just to lean against her and chew a piece of dried meat. Soon, fires were built and berry stew was bubbling in the coiled baskets. My mother rolled hot rocks into the hot baskets to get them boiling. It sure smelled good.

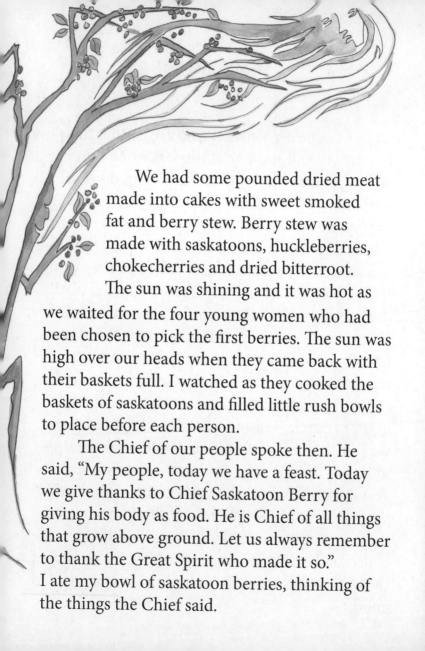

We had some pounded dried meat made into cakes with sweet smoked fat and berry stew. Berry stew was made with saskatoons, huckleberries, chokecherries and dried bitterroot.

The sun was shining and it was hot as we waited for the four young women who had been chosen to pick the first berries. The sun was high over our heads when they came back with their baskets full. I watched as they cooked the baskets of saskatoons and filled little rush bowls to place before each person.

The Chief of our people spoke then. He said, "My people, today we have a feast. Today we give thanks to Chief Saskatoon Berry for giving his body as food. He is Chief of all things that grow above ground. Let us always remember to thank the Great Spirit who made it so."

I ate my bowl of saskatoon berries, thinking of the things the Chief said.

We got up early the next morning, while it was still a little dark. The morning star was shining so bright. All the birds were singing good morning to us. We tied our bigger baskets to our backs and our little baskets to our waists in front. The saskatoon berry bushes were all heavy with berries. We walked from one bush to another, picking the berries.

"Chemai, come here, there are some big ones on this bush. Help me pick them, my basket is almost full," my friend called.

"Okay, Neekna, pretty soon all my baskets will be full, too," I said. I knew we would pick saskatoons for many days now. We would clean all the twigs and leaves out and spread them on tule mats in the hot sun to dry. We would have lots of sweet berries dried for winter.

One day my mother said, "Neekna, get your baskets ready and roll up a robe. We are going to ride to the high country to pick blackberries. Your father found a nice patch while he was hunting."

My heart jumped. I had never ridden a horse. I knew them all and walked alongside them when we travelled, but I had never sat on one. I ran to get my baskets.

"Chemai, Chemai, I'm going to ride with my mother. Come and watch me." Chemai came running out of her tipi.

"Oh, I wish I could come, too. Where are you going?"

My mother answered, "We are going to the high country to pick blackberries. We may camp one or two nights. We have room on my mother's horse if you want to come."

"Yes, aunt, I would like to do that. I'll tell my mother." Chemai ran to get her baskets.

We tied our baskets to the packs on the horse. My father, my brothers and some other men and women on horses came over to us.

"Hello, little berry pickers, do you want some help onto the horses?" We said, "Yes." They helped our mothers up, too. Chemai sat behind my grandma while I sat behind my mother.

My mother said, "Just hang on to my belt if you start bouncing around." It felt funny sitting way up there. Everyone seemed to be a lot shorter.

Great-grandma was there to say goodbye, too. She said, "Bring me lots of berries now. I like blackberries."

I said, "Tupa, look at me, now I'm like a bird," and she laughed and waved.

The climb did not take long, or maybe it just seemed faster because the horses did all the walking. I liked riding. Soon we were picking berries. The sweet blackberries covered the bushes everywhere. It didn't take long to fill my little basket.

"Come on, Chemai, let's empty our basket into the big one and move to another bush." Before the sun was even near the mountaintop, all the baskets were full, and my stomach was too. I was eager to go home.

"Tupa, look at all the blackberries we picked. They sure taste good. We picked some soapberries, too. Look in Mother's big basket. We are going to have some tonight with mashed blackberries." I pulled Tupa over to the baskets.

She said, "Oh my, I can hardly wait. I was hoping the soapberries would be ripe, too."

My mother said, "Come Neekna, we will gather some fresh branches and tie them together to make a beater for the soapberry food." I went with her and gathered twigs. We cleaned the leaves off them.

My mother mashed the soapberries into a coiled basket and added a little water. She used the bundle of twigs to swish and swish. Soon the mashed berries and water turned into a creamy foam. It grew and grew until it filled the basket. My mother then mashed the blackberries and mixed it into the creamy foam with her hand. It got stiffer and stiffer. When it finally had all turned to a stiff creamy foam, it was ready to eat.

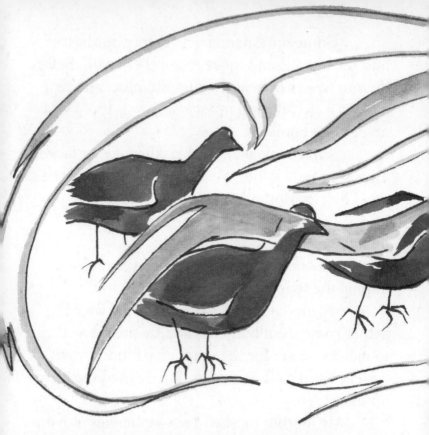

"Mmm, this is good, it's so sweet-bitter," my grandma said. I liked it, too. It was thick and creamy and tasted sweet, like the blackberries and a little bitter like the foamberries.

I really liked the moons of summer, because there were so many berries and roots to gather.

We could eat lots of it fresh. We also ate fresh trout
and grouse that our brothers and fathers brought
home. Chemai and I played in the water a lot, too.
We chased little ducks around. They were so funny.
They flapped their wings and went, "Kack, kack." I
wish this season would last and last.

Chapter 4
FALL

One morning, my father said, "Today we get ready to move to the Falls to wait for the salmon. The chokecherries will be good on the river banks. We will leave in the morning while it is still cool. By the time the sun hangs overhead, we will be there."

We gathered all of our things into big bundles and big tule-hemp bags. All day, everyone in the camp was busy. Chemai came rushing over to me.

"Neekna, are we going to ride?"

"No, Chemai, I already asked," I said. "We will walk, only Tupa will ride with all the bundles."

"Oh, it's not very far to the Falls anyway, it will be fun," Chemai said. Tupa sang lots of songs as we walked beside her horse. There were all kinds of things to see. We saw a groundhog just lying on a rock.

"Look, he is so fat he can't move," Chemai said. Of course he could move, he just looked like he couldn't. We even saw a coyote run across the trail ahead of us.

"Coyote, come back, we are friends," we called. However, he just trotted faster. He was probably looking for his brother Fox, just like in the stories we heard from our Tupa.

Before we arrived at the Falls, we could hear it. "Listen," said Tupa, "can you hear the Falls singing? It never stops. It sounds good, doesn't it?"

"Yes," we said. "What is it singing about?"

"It is singing about the fish that will come soon."

"It is singing about all the people who will gather to catch the salmon." It is happy. We were happy, also, to camp near the Falls.

One day, the men gathered. The Chief of our people spoke. He said, "I watch the water every day at the Falls. Today we will fish. I will send the young men to set the traps. Then we will feast on all the first salmon caught. After that, the salmon caught will be divided equally among the people for drying."

My grandmother said to us, "Our Chief is a good man. He knows that Salmon gave his body to everyone for food. All the salmon caught is shared equally, because only a certain number arrive each year. If one person took all the salmon for his family, where would the other families get some?" I knew that our Chief was a great man; no wonder he was greatly respected. We were lucky.

"Let's hang these fish, Neekna," Chemai said, "Don't they look good?"

"Yes," I answered. There were rows and rows of drying fish, hanging in the sun. We ran back and forth from our mothers to the drying racks, hanging the fish on slim poles. There was lots of work but it was fun. We would have lots of fish for winter. We already had big bags full of dried salmon and salmon eggs. I liked the eggs, especially when they were pounded into a powder and mixed with pounded saskatoon berries.

The days were a lot shorter now and the nights were crispy cool as we started back to our winter camp. We had to leave some of our bundles of food for the men to retrieve later. We had so much food of all kinds.

On the way my grandmother said, "Look, there is Rock Woman from the stories. She waits by the road for travellers. She is good to them and gives them luck if they give her a gift when they go by." The Rock Woman stood high on a bank. I went with my grandmother up to her. There were lots of things at her feet that people had left for her.

There were bone beads, shells, bird claws and coloured pieces of buckskin.

My grandmother said, "Let us give her these clam shells I have, they are pretty." We put them at her feet while my grandmother talked to Rock Woman.

"Many years ago, when only animal people were here, you were changed to a rock to watch over this valley, the Okanagan," she said. "We honour you today. You are much older than we will ever be. You have seen many things. You remind us of how short our time is here and how we are only a little part of a long line before and after us. You watch over our people as they travel up and down the Okanagan. You will be here many snows from now to see my great-great-grandchildren. Watch over them kindly, as you have watched over us. The Great Spirit who made you must have found you so lovely he placed you here, for many to see and honour."

I thought of Rock Woman and how long she had stood there and how much longer she would be there. I wondered who the people would be that she would see many snows from now. I hoped, I thought, they would honour her, too.

Back at our winter camp, we raced around and looked to see if everything was the same as we had left it. We climbed down into the pit house and chipmunks ran around chattering at us. We laughed.

"Look, Neekna, they made a nest in here. They must have lived in here all summer while we were gone. They're mad at us; they think it's their house now," Chemai said.

Last night, it was cold. This morning the ground was white with frost. The leaves were turning all colours on the trees. This is the season of fall.

"Your father should be home from hunting today," my mother told me. "Your sister and your grandma will be with them, they should have lots of dried meat and dried huckleberries. They've been gone almost ten days now. They went to the high country where lots of huckleberries grow and the deer and elk are plenty."

"I'm lonesome for my grandma. I do hope they will be back today," I said.

Soon they came riding into the camp. "Neekna, look, they have lots of big bundles," my mother said, her eyes looking happy. Everyone was back from hunting and food gathering. We had lots of food stored.

Our Chief said to us, "We will be having a feast of thanks for all the foods we have gathered. We will thank the four food Chiefs who gave their bodies up to feed us. First, there will be Chief Bitterroot, then Chief Saskatoon Berry, then Chief Salmon, and then Chief Bear.

Chief Bear is the greatest Chief of all, because he laid his life down first to make all the other Chiefs become food. He gave up his body so we would have meat of all kinds to eat. A special song of honour is sung each time a black bear is killed. This song is sung all day until sundown. This is done in thanks to the greatest of all the Chiefs.

"My people, remember this always. That is the way our people do certain things. We must honour our relatives, the animals, the fish and the plants that share their lives so that we may have life. If we do not honour them and forget how important they are to us, we begin to destroy them. If their lives are in danger, so are ours. That is the Law of the Giver of Life. Remember that always and remember to tell your grandchildren."

The feast of thanks was big. We all were sitting in a big circle around the food all the women prepared. I sat between my grandma and my grandpa. My mother was helping to serve the bowls of the four main foods. On my eating mat were all kinds of cooked meats, baked fish, black moss, steamed roots and powdered pine nuts.

I said to my grandma, "Can I start to eat?"

"No, you have to wait for your bowl of the four main foods," she said. "We will all pray together in thanks for the foods that come into our bodies and become us. That is how the plants, the fish and the animals are part of us. That is why we respect them. They are part of the big Circle that makes up everything. We are part of it, too. Now hold up your bowl of foods and think about the things I have told you. Think most of all about the Great One who made it so."

As I held up my bowl of the four main foods, I thought of all the things my Tupa, my grandma and my mother had told me and the things I had seen this whole year from the first season of the preparation to this ending season of thanks. I could see how all the things worked together and how we were part of it. I knew that we were living the way the Great One wanted us to. We used what He gave to us. We did not destroy or use things we did not need. Someone or something else might need it.

I knew now why my Tupa, my grandma, and my mother knew so much. They were told stories by their old ones, just like I was being told. Someday, I would tell my grandchildren the very same things and they would tell their grandchildren.

As long as we keep the respect for all things the Great One made, we will not have any hardship. That is the way it was planned. I thanked the Great One and all the great food Chiefs, for through their help, I could be here on this fine day.